A Suitable Husband

Jude Knight

Published by Jude Knight
Copyright 2017 Judith Anne Knighton writing as Jude Knight
Publisher: Titchfield Press

ISBN: 978-0-473-40306-5

Dedication

To the Bluestocking Belles, for whom I wrote this story. Thank you for inspiring, stretching, and supporting me.

A Suitable Husband

As the Duchess of Haverford's companion, Cedrica Grenford is not treated as a poor relation and is encouraged to mingle with Her Grace's guests. Perhaps among the gentlemen gathered for the duchess's house party, she will find a suitable husband?

Marcel Fournier has only one ambition: to save enough from his fees serving as chef in the houses of the ton to become the proprietor of his own fine restaurant. An affair with the duchess's dependent would be dangerous. Anything else is impossible. Isn't it?

Prologue

London
September 1812

Cedrica Grenford set her portable writing desk on the table. She had freshly prepared quills, a full bottle of ink, and neatly cut sheets of paper, each with the Haverford crest watermarked in the background. She took a deep breath and pushed her glasses farther up her nose. She was ready for this, her first test as confidential secretary and companion to Her Grace, the Duchess of Haverford.

That is to say, to Aunt Eleanor. Who would have thought that little Ceddie Grenford would grow up to one day call a duchess 'aunt'? Even if that illustrious personage was remotely connected by marriage.

She had not imagined such a result when she had written to the duke to beg a refuge for her father, his distant cousin, who was failing in health and confused in mind. Papa was an ill-paid country vicar with a lifetime habit of giving away whatever came into his hands. Now the church he had served so devotedly proposed to put him into a poorhouse. Or an asylum.

Two weeks ago, the duchess, escorted by her son, the Marquis of Aldridge, descended upon their house and carried Papa off to be cared for in a lovely pensioner cottage near Haverford Castle in Kent, taking Cedrica to London to serve the duchess as a companion. Of course, Cedrica had breathed a grateful sigh of relief… until this afternoon. She might be a little nervous, but she was determined to do well in her new role.

"Cedrica, my dear," said Her Grace, "come here and meet some of the ladies who form our committee."

Cedrica managed to acquit herself without disgrace as she was presented to some of the duchess's legion of goddaughters and their friends. Lady Emily Pembroke stopped her conversation with Lady de Courtenay to smile at Cedrica. Lady de Courtenay gave a friendly wave. Miss Sedgely offered a straightforward handshake, and Lady Elinor Lacey introduced the two bored schoolgirls with them as Miss Louise Durand and Miss Blanche Lacey.

The Belvoir sisters, Lady Sophia and Lady Felicity, also greeted Cedrica warmly. "I am to act as chairman, and Lady de Courtenay will make a third with you and I," Lady Sophia said. "This committee has much work to do, Miss Grenford, and the three of us most of all."

Lady Sophia introduced Miss Lockhart, who in turn made Miss Kate Woodville known to the company. Miss Woodville, it seemed, was a teacher at a young ladies' academy. Perhaps teaching might be a future for Cedrica. She would make a point of talking to the young woman.

"Aunt Eleanor, I brought my friend, Miss Baumann," Lady Felicity said, "Esther has a great interest in education for girls, and that is why we are here, is it not?"

The duchess smiled. "You must be Mr. Nathaniel Baumann's daughter, Miss Baumann. You are most welcome to our number. Shall we be seated, ladies?"

This is no different to taking notes for the meetings of the Ladies' Altar Society, or the Mothers' Union, or the Vestry. So Cedrica had been telling herself for days, but these were not farmers' wives and shopkeepers; these were fine ladies in fashionable silks with upper-class vowels and curious eyes.

And if the ladies were terrifying, the gentlemen would be worse. Lord Aldridge had suggested that she regard the proposed house party as an opportunity to meet a suitable husband and had promised to pay a dowry if such a gentlemen could be brought to propose. His money was safe enough. She preferred not even to speak to gentlemen of the ton if she could avoid it.

Cedrica sat in front of her desk, at the left hand of the duchess and the right of Lady Sophia, who took the head of the table and opened the meeting.

"Ladies, you know why we are here. Several of us were talking about the dearth of opportunities for women in all classes, should they want more of an education than the skills that our world deems 'appropriate for a woman.' We do not think ourselves less capable of great learning than our brothers, nor do we consider ourselves extreme examples of our kind. We believe that women who wish to study the arts or the sciences should be able to do so, as have some of us ourselves."

Goodness. Had such ideas been suggested at a Vestry meeting, the speaker would have been laughed out of the room, with her father leading the mirth.

Even the Ladies' Altar Society would have been shocked. But these grand ladies were all nodding, even Her Grace.

"But talk butters no parsnips," Lady Sophia continued. "We agreed that we needed a fund to support schemes for assisting girls to be educated beyond the sphere to which their sex, class, or both assign them. Her Grace has kindly agreed to be patroness of this fund and has an idea for announcing it to the world and, at the same time, raising money to support it. Ladies, you, your family and friends, and anyone who is in the least likely to support us are invited to Hollystone Hall in Buckinghamshire this December for a holiday house party and a New Year's Eve Charity Ball."

The explosion of delighted comments that filled the room flowed over Cedrica. A ball. How on earth would she ever manage that, much less the house party that would precede it?

Chapter One

Hollystone Hall, Buckinghamshire
November 1812

Marcel Fournier sat on the bed assigned to him in the wing set aside for upper servants at Hollystone Hall and brooded on his wrongs.

The house was grand enough, the house party would serve the highest in Society, and Marcel could certainly not complain about the wages he would receive for a mere month of employment. The Duchess of Haverford was also compensating him richly for the few days needed to visit the house this month so he could advise on the construction of the kitchen he would use for the three-week event.

And that was the sticking point.

Not the kitchen itself. They were building—had almost finished building—a whole new kitchen out of some unused storage rooms. He was thrilled and flattered to have final say on the selection and placement of equipment, from the modern iron range to the last pot and spoon. No. He had no complaints about the kitchen he already regarded as his own.

Even the need for a second kitchen; he could concede the sense of that. To him would fall the important task of preparing the banquets that would thrill and impress the guests each and every night, culminating in the dinner on the night of the grand ball that would end the house party. He and the servants set to assist him would have their hands full with dish after dish after dish, each one different and each magnificent.

Let the English cook have her own kitchen to make little scones and heavy cakes, to fry eggs, bacon, and sausages, for the lesser meals of the day.

But she should answer to him. He, Marcel Fournier, was the master chef. He was a former apprentice to the great Carême himself. He should be in charge of all menus, ruler of both kitchens, deciding what would be made and how the kitchen staff were to be allocated. What was this Cissie Pearce but a country cook?

"Good English cooking," Mademoiselle Grenford had said. "Mrs. Pearce is known for her good English cooking."

Marcel could do good English cooking! Had he not grown up here in England after his family escaped from the Terror?

In Spitalfields, until he was apprenticed to a cook in an inn on Tottenham Court Road, then in Soho where he took charge in an earl's kitchen, and finally, after having himself smuggled into France and attracting the man's attention by the bold trick of sneaking into his office with a box of his own *pâtisseries* and menus for a year's worth of banquets, in the kitchen and under the direct supervision of the great Marie-Antoine Carême, chef to Talleyrand and through him to the diplomats of Europe.

For the past two years, Marcel had been one of the most sought-after chefs in the whole South of England. Good English cooking, indeed.

She was a little dab of a thing, Mademoiselle Grenford, with her light brown hair pulled back into one of the unloveliest coiffures he had ever seen and her thick glasses concealing rather fine eyes. He had thought her a mouse and had tried to overwhelm her with his masculine authority, honed by years as undisputed master of a kitchen. "I shall be in charge, of course, Mademoiselle," he told her. "I am a trained chef and a man. Madame Pearce shall lead in her own kitchen, but both kitchens shall answer to me."

"The two kitchens shall operate independently, Monsieur Fournier," the little mouse replied calmly. "Each of you shall be responsible for your own kitchen, its staff, and the food it produces."

Whatever arguments he raised, however loudly, she just repeated the same thing. When Marcel Fournier was displeased, sous-chefs made themselves inconspicuous, apprentices cried, and kitchen maids fainted, but Mademoiselle Grenford just repeated, "The two kitchens shall operate independently," until he ran out of ire, and came to bed.

So what now? Did he continue to agitate to be master below stairs? Or should he tell the duchess that he would not take the commission? Cede the field and with it the lucrative rewards of the handsome fee he was being paid and the opportunity to impress potential clients for the restaurant he would one day open when his savings grew sufficiently?

Put like that, there was little choice. The English had a saying about cutting off one's nose to spite one's face. He preferred his nose to continue in its current position. Well then. In the morning, he would concede, and he would do so with flair. Madame Pearce would be grateful for his magnanimity. Mademoiselle Grenford would be impressed at his generosity.

Since he was staying, he would inspect his kitchen again. He had some ideas for improving the layout. He would note them tonight and instruct the little mademoiselle in the morning.

Marcel found his slate and some chalk and threaded through the dark halls. His candle threw insufficient light in the cavernous space that would, in less than a month, be a bustling center for gastronomic excellence. He retraced his steps to Mrs. Pearce's deserted domain and retrieved a whole box of candles.

Two hours later, his slate covered with notes and his head full of plans, he went to return the box. In the morning, he would astound the little mouse with his brilliance! But he stopped at the kitchen door. There, enveloped in a shawl over her nightrail, with her hair cascading over her shoulders, was Mademoiselle Grenford herself, her elbows on the table, a cup clasped between two hands.

Hot milk, perhaps? He could have made her hot milk, with a touch of nutmeg and perhaps a hint of honey to sweeten. Perhaps he should offer.

No. He would not disturb her.

Marcel took the image of her back to his room. She was a sweet little mouse, was Mademoiselle. Out of his orbit, of course. He hinted to clients of his elevated family, brought low by the revolution. The claims were fantasy. He had been born in a noble household, as he claimed, but his father was a valet, and his mother a dairy maid. La Grenford really was a lady of the nobility, and from a ducal family at that.

But he could ease her way in this coming house party, and he would.

As he prepared for bed, he imagined her expressions of delight as guest after guest complimented her on the fine cuisine and the smooth running of the dinner service. The large, comfortable bed would do very well for the month he would be in residence. Yes. The decision to stay was an excellent one.

He reached over to douse the candle but stopped. What was that noise? There it was again. A squeak? Had he conjured mice with his thoughts of the little mouse lady? But no, it was not a mouse squeak. More of a…

In seconds, he was out of bed and zeroing in on his travelling trunk, from which the sounds came, and what he saw there sent him running to the kitchen.

"Mademoiselle, you must come. You must come immediately. It is an outrage."

She looked up and blushed scarlet. "Monsieur! Your…" She turned her head away.

He looked down. He wore his shirt to bed, and nothing more, except a night cap against the cold. Coloring himself, he backed out the door. "I will dress, Mademoiselle. But quickly, and then you must come. A minute. No more."

Soon, with the cap shoved under a pillow and his shirt tucked into hastily donned pantaloons and covered by a banyan, he stood beside the lady looking down into the trunk, where a scrawny white cat fed a litter of newborn kittens. Inside his luggage. On his chef's caps and aprons.

"It is an outrage," he repeated a little helplessly. The cat was watching them through eyes slitted with the joys of motherhood and purring loudly enough to wake the household.

"This is Cristal, the housekeeper's cat," the mademoiselle said. "Mrs. Stanley will be pleased that you found her, Monsieur Fournier. She was worried."

"Found her? Worried? But she…" Running out of words, he scratched the cat behind one ear, and she purred more loudly.

"You keep an eye on her," the mouse commanded, "and I shall find a box in which to move her. Do not worry, Monsieur. I will see to it that your garments are laundered in the morning, and they shall be good as new."

And she whisked out of the room, leaving him guardian of the feline and her young and in possession of the memory of an exceedingly trim pair of ankles.

Chapter Two

Hollystone Hall, Buckinghamshire
18th December 1812

"Excuse me, miss."

Cedrica did not have to look up from her writing desk to recognize the person who had interrupted their meeting. It was Mrs. Pearce's assistant cook this time.

Two hours ago, she had been taken away from her inconspicuous supervision of the house party's first breakfast service by Monsieur Fournier's senior kitchen maid. Yesterday, amidst the hustle of arrivals, no fewer than five inter-kitchen battles had broken out and needed mediation. And four the day before. And six the day before that.

Since Monsieur Fournier and his coach-loads of ingredients and equipment had taken up residence five days ago, the troubles between the two kitchens had been Cedrica's biggest headache, dwarfing her concerns about bedchamber allocation, seating plans, and spreading the services of the team of maids and valets among those who had arrived without servants.

"Oh dear," commiserated Grace, Lady de Courtenay. "Another shot fired in the kitchen war?"

"I am sorry, miss. It's the large soup tureen, miss. Mrs. Pearce says she needs it, and that Frenchie, he has it in his kitchen and won't give it up, never so." Aggie Wilkins nodded firmly, her message delivered.

"We are almost done." Lady Sophia Belvoir blotted the paper on which she had been neatly writing notes about the day's activities. "I shall report to Aunt Eleanor, ladies. Shall we check with one another here at," she consulted her notes, "two of the clock?"

Sophia had been right that the three of them would have the most work of all. Each led a team of volunteers to manage some part of the party: Sophia in charge of all the casual activities that would be available for guests to enjoy, Grace the many more formal events, and Cedrica the domestic matters such as food and bed linen. They had all arrived early to have the house in readiness, and every day, they would meet several times to make sure the organization was, as Her Grace insisted, both invisible and seamless.

Grace patted Cedrica's hand. "Cedrica, do you need help?"

Cedrica smiled, grateful for the offer. "I can do it."

In truth, Cedrica would rather be managing the kitchen staff than the grand ladies and gentlemen who fell into Grace's and Sophia's purview. She could talk easily with those below stairs and resolve their arguments, too. Cedrica was a veteran of the 1809 war between Widow Siddons and Miss Martha Ridley over the flower arrangements for the Easter ceremonies. Monsieur Fournier and Mrs. Pearce were child's play compared to those two ladies.

"One wonders whether the man's talent is worth his temperament," Sophia observed.

"After last night's dinner?" Grace asked.

Sophia acknowledged the point. "It was exceptional, was it not?"

"To be fair," Cedrica told them, "Mrs. Pearce is as bad. She has originated at least half the quarrels. Come, Wilkins, you shall tell me all about this soup tureen on the way below stairs."

The tureen lived, apparently, in one of the service pantries that the two kitchens reluctantly shared. Mrs. Pearce decided that the massive piece, which sat on its own warming burner, would be ideal for the potato and leek soup, served with crusty fresh bread, that would be one of the dishes offered in the less formal of the two dining rooms during the afternoon.

But the maid sent to fetch it returned empty handed, and further investigation disclosed that Monsieur Fournier had chosen it for the crème de champignons soup that was on the menu for dinner. He found it first, he said, and Mrs. Pearce would have to choose another tureen.

"But it's the spirit lamp, miss, see?" Mrs. Pearce explained. "Could be two hours that soup will be out, 'cause they don't all come in together, do they? Many of the ladies will sleep in and come down around noon, and some have broken their fast already, and won't want to eat till later. Most of the gentlemen have gone out for birds, and they'll want summat hot when they come in. Could be any time."

"Are there not other tureens with their own warmers? Or stands with spirit lamps you could put other tureens on?"

Mrs. Pearce reluctantly agreed there might be, but then rejected those they found. These were too small, and would lose heat too quickly. Those did not fit properly together. And that lot were not what she'd like to see in a duchess's dining room, and that was a fact.

"The big tureen is perfect, miss. And he don't need it, not really."

Cedrica sighed. "I shall go and see this wonderful tureen for myself, Mrs. Pearce. No, you do not need to come with me. I shall return and let you know what I have decided."

When she entered Monsieur Fournier's kitchen, he pretended to ignore her, though his gaze slid sideways and met hers for a second. Very well, let him carry on instructing some hapless undercook in the correct way to bone a swan. She was not waiting on his attention like a supplicant.

The disputed tureen was on a table on the far side of the room. He would notice her soon enough if she picked it up and started to carry it off! Not that she could even if she wished to. It was nearly large enough to bathe in and would need two people at least to lift it. She pushed at one handle, put her strength behind her hand, and managed to hoist the monstrous piece an inch or so.

It was a fine piece, she had to admit—fluted and curved, edged with scrolls and plaits of silver, polished to a mirror finish, and rearing majestically from the tiled warmer platform with not one but three burners to keep the soup hot.

But her eyes began to twinkle as she considered actually using it as part of a dinner service.

"Something is amusing, Mademoiselle?"

Monsieur Fournier had moved up beside her, the soft slippers he wore making no sound on the slate floor.

Cedrica blinked rapidly, determined not to show she was startled. "I came to solve your problem, Monsieur."

He gave a theatrical shrug, his hands widespread. "I have no problem, Mademoiselle. La Pearce has a problem. Not I."

"You are in the right, Monsieur. You were first to the tureen. It will look magnificent full of your wonderful mushroom soup. Only…" She allowed her voice to trail off and bent over to examine the platform more closely. Were the feet lion's paws? She rather thought they were.

Monsieur Fournier's hand appeared in her view, tapping on the table. He had long, rather elegant fingers, with neatly trimmed nails. He said nothing, but Cedrica could wait him out. And he proved no more immune to silence than a naughty choir boy caught with a broken window, an angelic smile, and a sling in his back pocket.

"You say, 'only', Mademoiselle? You will not judge in my favor despite your grand words?"

"Oh no, Monsieur. I cede you the tureen. If you wish to use it. Only…"

"'Only' again? Bah! What is this 'only'?"

She turned to lean against the table and smiled at him, trying to keep from laughing aloud. "Monsieur, it is very heavy, and we have fifty-six to dinner tonight. More, perhaps, if all those who are promised for the next two days arrive. How will you convey to them their soup? It is heavy even empty. Once it is full of soup…"

Monsieur Fournier's mouth dropped open, and he looked aghast at the magnificent tureen.

"I know," Cedrica said wickedly. "We could put it in a wheelbarrow, and the footmen could take it from guest to guest so that—"

She got no further. The chef's face darkened, and he roared, "A wheelbarrow? A wheelbarrow? You mock me, Mademoiselle!" He glared at the tureen. "A wheelbarrow, indeed!" He blinked, and his lips twitched. "The footmen could take it from guest to guest…" He began to chuckle and could barely get the last word out, "…in a wheelbarrow!"

The kitchen servants stopped what they were doing to stare as Monsieur Fournier roared with laughter, and Cedrica could not hold in her own amusement, until both of them were clutching the table with tears rolling down their cheeks.

At last, Monsieur Fournier collected himself, using the corner of his apron to wipe his eyes. As Cedrica used a kerchief for the same purpose, he asked, "And will you propose a wheelbarrow to Mrs. Pearce, Mademoiselle?"

"It is a different case, Monsieur. The monster here can be set up on the serving board ahead of time and filled with hot soup from buckets. Then the guests will go to the tureen themselves as they come to find sustenance a few at a time. For the dinner, though, we want something altogether grander, do we not? Four matching tureens, perhaps, each carried by a footman to a different part of the table, and the soup served from there. Or eight, marching in procession. Can I find you eight matching tureens, I wonder?"

Monsieur Fournier bowed elegantly. "Mademoiselle, you are as wise as you are beautiful. Let Madame Pearce have this monster. I, Marcel Fournier, will present the most delicious crème de champignons that England has ever tasted in a procession of eight tureens."

As Cedrica left to search the storerooms for matching tureens that would be worthy of the finest mushroom soup ever made in England, she heard the chef chuckling to himself in between barking orders at the undercooks. "Wheelbarrows! Was there ever such a woman?"

Chapter Three

It began with a set of ice molds.

Marcel planned a spectacular centerpiece for the second remove at tomorrow night's dinner—Italian creams made with eggs, rich cream, and a variety of fruits and other flavors molded into flower shapes, frozen, and then presented on a mountainous tower of ice, itself with pillars and platforms molded into fantasy shapes.

The Italian creams were made and stored in the estate's ice house. He sent an assistant to fetch the box containing the carved wooden mold for the tower. "Open it," he commanded. "Check that you have the correct box. The one I require has dolphin shapes to support the first tier."

But the assistant returned empty handed. "Monsieur, I cannot find the box with the dolphins."

He knew straight away of course, and a visit to Madame Pearce's kitchen soon confirmed it. The encroaching woman had taken the mold and intended to use the larger shapes for a salmon aspic!

Marcel tried to be reasonable. He really did. He could fill the molds with water this evening, and they would be set hard when the time came for setting up the display tomorrow. But Madame Pearce refused to consider it. Her salmon aspic was also for tomorrow and must remain in the molds until just before serving, or it would lose sharpness and definition.

"Then choose another set of molds, Madame," he suggested. "A set that is not a foundation piece of an entire tower."

The woman smirked. "You find something else. I got these ones first. That is what you said yesterday, Moosewer, when you refused to give up the waffle iron."

They had both wanted the waffle iron with the flower impression, but the mansion's shelves held three others equally pretty. He had found only one tower mold, and Madame Pearce did not even plan to make a tower! She could use any one of dozens of molds and make as lovely an aspic.

Marcel explained this to her, slowly, using simple words.

"You don't need to look down your long French nose at me, Moosewer," Madame Pearce told him. "I know I could use else, just like you could of yesterday. And I don't want to. Just like you yesterday."

He had promised Mademoiselle Grenford not to shout at Madame Pearce and not to swear at her in French. Or English. He had promised. He turned on his heel and marched away before he strangled the stubborn woman.

"Good riddance," Madame yelled after him.

Marcel went straight upstairs to the mademoiselle. At this time of day, she would be in the little sitting room where she and the other ladies of her committee had their meetings.

Once he left the service stairs for the main hallway, he set a bland look on his face and walked with determination. He passed several guests who ignored his existence, as he had expected. Servants should not be seen unless wanted, and therefore they would not see him.

Now. Around this corner and the fourth door on the right. Or was it the third?

He slowed, uncertainly. The third door was slightly ajar, and he could hear women's voices. Not the little mouse's, but those of the two ladies who were also helping to manage the house party.

"Lady Stanton is a difficult woman." That was the pretty young widow, Lady de Courtenay.

"Lady Stanton is a cold-hearted bitch." Lady Sophia Belvoir, the goddaughter of the duchess.

Marcel smiled a little. Who knew a lady would use such words? Deserved, undoubtedly. Even he, keeping though he did to his own domain, had heard stories of maids reduced to tears and footmen to helpless rage by the lady they named.

But the next words sobered him instantly.

"Do not cry, Cedrica. You are doing wonderfully well, and the duchess knows it. Lady Stanton will receive no support there."

Cedrica? That cold-hearted bitch had upset his mademoiselle?

"I agree with Grace, Cedrica. Aunt Eleanor shall give one of her deadly little set-downs, and I should dearly like to see it. Here. Dry your eyes, darling. It shall all be well, you will see."

Then the mademoiselle's voice sounded, trembling with unshed tears. "You are right. I know you are. I do not know why I allowed her to upset me so. Only I am so tired of stupid conflict. This gentleman does not want to share a room with his wife. That one has kept every guest in his wing awake with his snoring. This lady cannot have the same breakfast as that one, and another must be served the identical tray, right down to the color of the inlay. And as for the war between the kitchens! I swear, if I have to referee one more battle over who has first use of the lemon zester, I shall scream."

Really? She was not enjoying their little dramas as much as the two combatants? Marcel frowned and shot a glance both ways down the hallway to make sure he was not observed as he leaned closer. The two other ladies were making soothing noises and offering to take up the mademoiselle's duties while she rested.

"No, no. Aunt Eleanor would be so disappointed in me. Besides, you have your own tangles to straighten. Making sure that Lady Stanton and her cronies are not in a position to bully Miss Baumann, that Lord Trevor is dissuaded from taking out a gun, since he cannot see beyond the end of his arm and refuses to wear glasses, and that Lady Marchand can only cheat at cards with those who know her little ways."

The three ladies laughed together, Mademoiselle's chuckle still a little watery.

Her voice was forlorn when she added, "It was the other that hurt most, you know, because it is true."

More soothing noises, which she rejected.

"No. I am not a fool. I know that I have dwindled into an old maid. Well, look at me. Plain ordinary Cedrica Grenford. A useful person to have on a committee, but not one man has ever looked at me twice nor is likely to. I know Aunt Eleanor thinks dressing me up like a fashion doll and sending me in to talk to all these lords will turn me into a… a swan. But I am just a plain barnyard hen when you come down to it."

Lady de Courtenay disagreed. "Oh, but surely Lord Hythe—"

Another heart-wrenching chuckle. "See, his sister is shaking her head. And you are right, Sophia. Hythe is polite to everyone, and kind to me because I was at school with Felicity. He treats me as a lady, which is nice of him when I am, as Lady Stanton so kindly pointed out, merely hanging onto gentility by the charity of Her Grace."

"Oh, Cedrica…" That was both ladies.

Marcel's response to Lady Stanton's cruel words would have been much more forceful.

"He does not look at me and see a woman. No one does."

Lady Sophia spoke decisively. "You are blue-devilled, my dear. Who knows whether any of us will meet a man who can see past our elderly exteriors to the treasures we all are? If we do not, you and I shall be old maids together."

"Yes," Lady de Courtenay agreed. "Perhaps we should set up house together. Certainly Sophia and I have no more wish to live forever on the sufferance of our brothers than you do on the Haverfords'. Who needs men, after all? Selfish, conceited creatures, always jumping to conclusions."

This time, Mademoiselle Grenford's laugh was more genuine.

Lady Sophia said, "Rest for an hour. Read a book. I will order a pot of tea and some cakes, and Grace and I shall deal with anything that arises." Her voice was coming closer.

Swiftly, before she could open the door and find him listening, Marcel retreated down the hall and around the corner, all the way back downstairs, thinking furiously.

First, he must order a tray set with the most delicate of cups, the finest tea, and some of the little cakes from the test batch he had made that morning, in preparation for the real challenge of Christmas Day's dinner. Each was a work of art with its own sugar flower, and it had not escaped his notice that his mademoiselle liked them.

Then, while his assistants made the tray, he must make peace. This war must end. If that meant giving Madame Pearce her way on the tower, then so be it. He could not be part of causing pain to his mademoiselle.

His! How foolish he was. He was a chef. She was an aristo, of a family with a duke, despite her humble words. Yet *un chien regarde bien un évêque*. A dog can take a good look at a bishop. The English proverb was similar. A cat may look at a king. What would Mademoiselle Grenford think if she knew Marcel saw her as a woman, as she put it?

Perhaps bread to go with the cakes? Bread sliced thinly and buttered by his own hand and topped by some of Madame's conserve. A peace offering from them both.

Determined, he gave his orders to his kitchen and braved the kitchen of Madame Pearce. An odd quest, but would not a knight dare anything, brave any danger, undergo any humiliation, for the lady he must adore from afar?

Chapter Four

Christmas Day, 1812

If one more person arrived, they would need to sleep in the stables. Every room in the house was full, and the under servants were sleeping several to a bed.

Cedrica could not help a guilty thank you to whatever impulse set Mr. Arbuthwick climbing a tree to retrieve Miss Ellison's parasol, blown there by a stray gust of wind. He insisted that ice on the branches led to his fall, but Cedrica suspected a contribution from the warming punch he and his friends had been passing around.

Perhaps his relaxed state was for the best, as he suffered nothing worse than a sprained ankle. He was conveyed to the nearby town where his parents lived, to convalesce in the care of his fond mama, Miss Ellison's offer of nursing services having been vetoed by her own mother.

But Mr. Arbuthwick's room had not been empty above seventeen hours before Viscount Elfingham turned up at the door begging shelter. Yesterday, it was. Christmas Eve. He claimed his horse was lame, but Sophia confided that he was pursuing Felicity and that Hythe said it would not do.

Before the day was over, the sons of the duchess had also arrived. Lord Aldridge had been expected, but Lord Jonathan Grenford was thought to be somewhere in Russia. His mama was delighted, of course, but if Lord Jonathan had not cheerfully pronounced himself willing to sleep on a trundle in the room set aside for his brother, Cedrica did not know where she would have put him.

And now, on Christmas Day, another late arrival. Thank goodness Lord Elfingham did not object to sharing his room with Mr. Halevy! Mr. Halevy seemed a very nice gentleman, polite, not fussy, and with a charming French accent that reminded her of Monsieur Fournier. Although hearing him speak disproved one of the theories she had developed to explain her inconvenient fascination with the chef. The accent was clearly not the cause. She felt no such attraction to Mr. Halevy.

She left the new guest to the care of his room host and the servant allocated to valet far too many gentlemen for efficient service. What had seemed a large staff of servants was stretched almost to breaking point now the house was at capacity. To make things worse, Her Grace had declared that the servants were to work shortened hours today and a half day tomorrow, but her guests still wanted their breakfasts served, their clothing brushed, their chins shaved, their bath water carried, their corsets tightened, their forgotten gloves fetched, and on and on and on. So all day yesterday and today, Cedrica and Mrs. Stanley the housekeeper had been trying to juggle hours and people to perform the impossible.

The kitchens, her greatest trial in the early days of the house party, had become a haven, and she headed there now. She would just check that all was running smoothly for the second most important dinner of the whole event. And she would do so by way of the servants' stairs, thus avoiding the kissing boughs that Sophia and her decorating crew had hung everywhere. Cedrica had already been saluted by Hythe, Weasel Winderfield, and Lord Jonathan, and could not quite see the attraction of the pastime.

Since the kitchens had stopped sending for her several times a day, she had evolved the habit of visiting in the morning after the breakfast service and her meeting with Grace and Sophia. She took a cup of tea in one kitchen or the other, consulted with Mrs. Stanley, and admired whatever plans Mrs. Pearce and Monsieur Fournier had for the house party's meals. Frequently, she was called upon to sample some delicacy while its originator watched anxiously. She had no idea what had happened to the war, but the two kitchen heads were now firm friends, each bending over backward to help the other succeed.

Mrs. Pearce was alone when Cedrica arrived. Cedrica was not disappointed. Not at all. She was here to work, not to ogle Monsieur Fournier, however ogle-worthy he might be.

"No monsieur today?" she found herself asking.

"A busy day for Mark today, miss."

The words Monsieur, Fournier, and Marcel all being too difficult for Mrs. Pearce's tongue, she had taken to calling her colleague Mark.

"He gave permission for those who wished to go to the Christmas service, but of course that has put him behind and not many hours now until Christmas dinner."

Cedrica felt guilty. "Did Monsieur Fournier not wish to go to the Christmas service himself, Mrs. Pearce?"

"No church for his kind here, miss. He's a papist, see? French, of course. Lots of them are papists, so I hear. He's a nice boy for all that, and a good chef. He'll get his ordinary, right enough."

"'His ordinary?'" Was that a kind of award for chefs? Or something to do with being French? Or Catholic? It was not clear from Mrs. Pearce's speech which of the two made his niceness a surprise.

"You know, miss. A French ordinary in London. A place for the gentlemen to have their dinners. It's what Mark wants, why he is taking jobs like this instead of a proper position in a house, like me. Good experience, good contacts, and good money, Mark says."

Cedrica's spurt of resentment was most unreasonable. Monsieur Fournier was free to confide in his fellow cook if he wished. And Cedrica's life was calmer now the two were friends.

"Go and say hello, miss," the cook urged. "He'd appreciate the interest, I'm sure."

"I would not want to disturb him when he's busy."

"We're all busy today, miss, you as much as the rest of us, I'll be bound." Mrs. Pearce and her staff would be serving Christmas dinner in the servants' hall. Three times: once for her own kitchen staff and the outdoor servants, once for the upstairs servants when their masters and mistresses went down to dinner, and once and finally for Monsieur Fournier's kitchen.

And Cedrica, as soon as she put her nose above stairs, would be pounced on by a guest with a problem only she could solve. Indeed, even here, the housekeeper or the under butler might track her down. They would not trespass in Monsieur Fournier's kitchen, especially when the temperamental chef was under such pressure. He would not have time to make her a cup of the coffee she had come to enjoy since being taken up by the duchess, but perhaps she could just sit for a minute or two and watch other people work.

The kitchen was as chaotic as she had expected. She took a chair at the end of the kitchen table farthest from all of the activity, and a few minutes of careful observation disclosed the order and patterns of frantic movement centered on Monsieur who stood, the calm center of a purposeful storm: barking orders, giving advice, tasting from spoons and plates that anxious disciples brought to him.

A hand appeared over her shoulder, a cup of coffee, followed by another with a plate of the small cakes Monsieur decorated with such artistry. She smiled at the maidservant who was placing it for her, but the girl nodded toward Monsieur, who caught Cedrica's gaze for a moment, smiled, then turned back to the next in his line of supplicants.

She took a sip. Hot, creamy, and sweet. Just as she liked it.

Moments later, Monsieur Fournier joined her, hooking a chair with one foot and sitting on it back to front so he could rest one arm along the top rail while he sipped his own black, bitter brew. "Is there something I can do for you, Mademoiselle Grenford?"

"No, no. I had no wish to disturb you, Monsieur Fournier. I just wished to sit for a minute and not be interrupted. I can go."

He put a hand on her arm to stop her rising and snatched it back as if he, too, felt the shock of that connection." My kitchen is your refuge. I am honored, and only sorry it is so…" He shrugged helplessly, an expressive lift of his shoulders and a wave of his free hand.

"It is nice," Cedrica confided, "to see everyone working and not to be responsible for any of it."

He smiled. She had noticed before how the smile transformed his lean dark face, making it seem much younger. "I am responsible for them, and to you, Mademoiselle."

"To the duchess, surely."

"Oh no." He stared at the coffee cup as if it held the secrets of the universe. "To you, Mademoiselle, make no mistake." His dark lashes swept up, and his eyes, dark as his coffee, looked deep into hers. "My kitchen, my craft, my service. All are devoted to you, Mademoiselle Grenford." He pushed himself to his feet, flushing slightly. "I should not have spoken. I am tired, I think. Forgive me, Mademoiselle. You need not fear that I will embarrass or importune you. I know my place."

A loud crash startled Cedrica and drew Monsieur Fournier from her side to berate the boy who had darted through the door without looking just as a maid crossed the room with a stacked pile of serving bowls.

Cedrica sat and sipped until her cup was empty, hoping he would come back, but he did not look at her again, returning instead to conducting the work of the kitchen, and in the end she went back upstairs, where she did not belong any more than she belonged down here.

What good did it do knowing he was attracted to her as she was to him? He was right, of course. The duchess would never countenance such a connection. It was impossible.

Wasn't it?

Chapter Five

I *should not be doing this.*

Marcel flicked a non-existent speck of dust from the pristine folds of his extravagantly lacy cravat and frowned at his reflection in the small mirror that was all his room afforded.

I should definitely not be doing this.

On the other hand, who was to know? He wore a mask and would assume an English accent. If his French intonations seeped through, his costume would provide an excuse—he sounded French, because he was Louise XIV, the great French king. In any case, who would expect to see the duchess's chef dressed as *le Roi-Soleil* and dancing with her guests?

One guest. Or not a guest. A member of the family, rather.

For just one dance with her, I will risk all.

He doffed his tricorne hat as he bowed, the red-dyed ostrich plumes tossing gently.

Cissie Pearce had found the costume and had encouraged him to dare the masquerade. "What harm can it do? And don't you worry none about the supper, Mark. You have it all ready, and I can watch your people."

Was it a costume? Or something a former duke had worn? A white silk shirt with hugely puffed sleeves gathered to lacy cuffs, gold breeches tied below the knee over red stockings, a richly embroidered knee-length waistcoat, open from the waist, and, over it all, an ornately brocaded robe that just missed sweeping the ground as he stood. The cravat, buckled shoes, and a carved walking stick with a gold tip made up the rest of the costume. The wig had been in a different part of the attic but worked well enough: black, curly, and long enough to drape across his shoulders.

He answered the tap on the door cautiously, removing his hat and opening just wide enough that the visitor would see nothing but his head. It was Cissie, and he opened wider to let her in.

"Well, look at you." Cissie was all admiration, clucking over the fine lace and the perfect fit of the shoes. "Let's see you with your mask on. There. You're that fine, Mark. Now be off with you, and don't worry about a thing. Ain't nobody up here but us, and if you go out down the main stairs, no one will know any different, but you're a guest of the house."

Swept along on her confidence, he found himself approaching the rooms where a bare three hours earlier he had been one of the servants setting up for the duchess's costume party.

The rooms were full of kings and queens, gods and goddesses, Roman soldiers and cavaliers. Ah. There she was. One solitary shepherdess hovering in the supper room, keeping watch over the comings and goings of the servants.

The fates favored him. In the next room, the musicians began to play a waltz. Did he dare dance it as the current mode was in Paris? Yes. Ladies were taking the floor in the arms of their partners. Within minutes, he could be embracing his dear mademoiselle, albeit only on the dance floor. His breath caught at the mere thought.

Mademoiselle Grenford looked up as he approached, tipping her head a little to one side as she waited for him to speak.

"May I have the honor of this dance, fair shepherdess?" he asked.

She furrowed her brows for the briefest of seconds. "I do not dance, sir, but I will find you a partner—"

"Not dance? When your costume is made to swirl on the dance floor, and the music begs—nay, demand—for you to pay homage?" A slip there. He had pronounced homage in the French way.

Her eyes widened, but she said nothing, merely— oh joy—placed her gloved hand in his and allowed herself to be conducted through the doors to join the waltz.

They began slowly, his hands resting tentatively just above her waist, and hers placed lightly on his shoulders. He honored the respectable distance due to a maiden, but as they began to circle one another in the dance, his legs shifted past hers and could not avoid repeated touching.

Turn, turn, and turn again. The candles of the chandeliers seemed to whirl above them, the other dancers disappeared, and he and Mademoiselle Grenford were alone in the ballroom. She swayed and dipped and twirled with him, light as a feather but far more substantial, a delight to his hands, his arms, and his legs.

Her eyes fixed on his, her face flushed, she murmured, "Monsieur Fournier, what are you doing here?"

It was a dose of cold water, jerking him back to reality. Would she rebuke him? Tell the duchess?

"One dance," he managed, almost begged. "I promised not to importune you, Mademoiselle, but I thought… In costume, no one would know if I stole one dance."

Somehow, his feet kept moving, they kept dancing, round and round and round, their legs shifting past each other's again and again, their eyes still locked.

She smiled, a benison beyond his deserving. "This dance is not a theft, Monsieur, when I give it willingly."

"Give?"

He was in heaven. He was no longer dancing; he was floating several inches about the ballroom floor. *She knows me even in my disguise. She dances with me willingly.*

His heart was too full for speech, and she said nothing more as they continued around the floor, oblivious to everything except the music and one another.

Marcel stepped back when the music ended, dropping his hands from her waist to her hands, unable to resist touching her for a moment more. "Thank you, Mademoiselle. Thank you more than I can say. I will leave now, but you have given me food for many happy dreams."

"No." Mademoiselle Grenford folded her fingers around his and tugged him to follow her. By chance, they had stopped at the most poorly lit end of the ballroom, close to the corner where a door let on to a servant's passage, and it was to this she marched determinedly, with Marcel bobbing after in her wake.

No. Not that door. She was opening a door onto the terrace, and in moments, they were outside.

"I do not want it to end," she said. "Will you not consent to sit and talk with me for a little?"

Consent? Did she not know he would consent to the guillotine for her sake?

"But you will be cold! Here." He struggled out of his heavy robe and wrapped it around her, but she protested when she saw his arms unprotected by no more than the silk of his shirtsleeves.

"We shall share it," she proposed as she guided him through an arch into one of the hedged gardens and then to a hidden stone seat tucked into an arbor that in summer would be fragrant with roses.

It is a dream. I am asleep in my bed and dreaming of sitting here in the duchess' garden, sharing a robe with my mademoiselle. It is a dream, and I hope I never awaken.

She had commanded talk. What could he talk about? "Did the tenants like their gifts, Mademoiselle?"

They were wasteful, the aristos, with much food left after every meal. Mademoiselle had agreed it should go to those in need, and she and the duchess had asked for some of the finer dishes to be saved for the gifts traditionally given to the poor on St. Stephen's Day. Marcel had taken great care with the selection and the presentation in baskets.

For a time, he listened, commenting just enough to keep her talking as she told him about the trip she had made yesterday with the duchess and some of the other ladies.

"You have a generous heart, Monsieur," she finished. "That is what my father used to say. Some give reluctantly out of duty. You can tell those with generous hearts because they take pleasure in the happiness of those who receive."

He shrugged. "I have been hungry, Mademoiselle. When I was a little boy, after my family fled France, we had very little. I do not forget."

"Will you feed the poor of London with the leftovers from your Ordinary once you have it?"

"Did the excellent Cissie tell you of my plans? But she is wrong, you know. I do not plan a French *Ordinaire*, Mademoiselle. Say, rather, *Extraordinaire*. As they have in France. *Un restaurant*, Mademoiselle, with the finest cuisine listed on a menu from which patrons can choose, an excellent cellar, a quiet setting— perhaps with music playing, prompt and efficient service. A place where gentlemen would be proud to bring their guests or could dine alone without the expense of keeping a kitchen and a chef."

Now it was his turn to spin out the words, while she asked quiet questions, her eyes turned up to his in the light of the quarter moon.

"And so I take work wherever I can find it, Mademoiselle, and one day, I will have sufficient money, and *Fournier's of London* will open for business," he finished.

Marcel fell silent. The moon would set soon. They would need to go in while it still gave enough light to find their way without falling into one of the moats or ponds. He did not want the dream to end.

Mademoiselle echoed his thoughts. "We need to go. It will be full dark when the moon goes down."

Marcel stood reluctantly, and she stood with him, still in the warmth of his coat.

"It is cold, Monsieur," she said. "Keep the robe around us both until we are inside."

So he put his arm around her to help them walk in harmony, and—oh, magical night—she put her arm around him. Marcel said nothing as they walked slowly back to the house. He was soaking up the warmth of her, the curves of her, the way she fitted neatly under his arm.

He could not resist. Even one of God's saints would have done it, and Heaven knew, Marcel was no saint. As they rounded the corner that concealed the door, he stopped and used his other hand to turn her toward him. Naturally, she looked up.

Her lips were as sweet as he had imagined, and she did not draw back and slap his impertinent face. Far from it. She pressed herself into the kiss, and though she was untutored in the art, she learned quickly. Marcel was left reeling when at last a burst of noise from inside the ballroom intruded, and they parted.

"Mademoiselle—" he began.

"Don't." Mademoiselle put up a hand to stop his mouth, and he kissed her fingers. "Don't spoil it by apologizing." She stood within his arms, but he could feel she was poised to flee, and he had no idea what to say or do.

A moment, and it was too late. She stretched up, gave him a swift peck on the lips, and slipped away from under his robe. Marcel watched, his hand touching the lips she had so favored as she opened the door and returned to the party.

It is over, then, but more, so much more than I ever imagined.

He would not go back inside. He would find his way to his kitchen and become a chef once more. And this night would be forever a jewel to carry in his heart.

Chapter Six

New Year's Eve

That was it?

One magical dance? One enchanted hour in the moonlight? One kiss that thrilled her to the soles of her feet and left her tingling even days later?

And then nothing?

Perhaps not quite nothing, for his eyes followed her whenever she entered his realm, intent and sad. But whatever else she had expected, it had not happened. No declaration. No stolen moments. No whispered avowals of regard.

He behaved as if their time together had not happened and not changed the complexion of the entire world, destroying even her haven in his kitchen. No longer did she relax when she sat at the table watching the kitchen servants scurrying to his command. Far from it.

Being in the same room with him was painful. Her heart ached, and not just her heart. She had but to look at him to remember the touch of his lips, his hands, his body pressed against hers. Memories were pale ghostly substitutes for the real thing but enough to have her stirring restlessly and cutting her visits short.

Not that she had much time to brood. With most of the ladies' committee succumbing to Cupid's assault and absorbed in their suitors, Cedrica was busier than ever. Even her co-hosts had fallen victim. Sophia had left yesterday to join Lord Elfingham in London and, Cedrica hoped, would marry him there, and Grace had made up her quarrel with her Lord Nicholas and spent every moment she could with him.

Cedrica co-opted Esther Baumann to help. Esther's courtship had prospered, but her suitor had returned to London so giving her work to do was a kindness.

Esther was in the small sitting room that Sophia had dubbed the Command Tent, writing letters to every house with pretensions to gentility within a two-hour ride of Hollystone Hall. She looked up as Cedrica joined her. "Almost done," she said. "If all these people agree, we shall be able to billet half of Society on the neighbors."

"Which is to the good, Esther, for I swear Her Grace has invited the better part of Society, and if they all come, we shall be inviting dukes and earls to share their horses' beds!"

"It will not be as bad as that," the duchess soothed, startling Cedrica who had not heard her enter the room. "Most of them are too far away to travel for a single night's entertainment, but if they send a bank note for our Fund, I shall be pleased enough."

The size to which the fund had grown was astounding, far outstripping the colossal amount the duchess had spent on the house party, but the New Year's Eve Ball would bring in as much again, with each guest paying for their ticket and further opportunities to donate in the course of the evening.

"There." Esther blotted the letter she had been writing. "That is the last. I shall see to these being delivered." She gathered up the bundle of sealed letters and went to find the senior footman whose job it was to send grooms to the neighbors with Her Grace's missives.

The duchess took a seat by the window and gestured for Cedrica to join her. Her Grace had not been in this room since before the house party, contenting herself with daily reports and quick consultations wherever she happened to be during the day. Whoever did the bulk of the work, Cedrica was in no doubt that Her Grace was firmly in charge of the entire event, knew exactly what went on under her roof, and would step in if the ladies made a decision that was not to her liking.

Had that happened? Had she done something the duchess disapproved of?

"Did you need me for something, Aunt Eleanor?"

The duchess' reply was cryptic. "I think perhaps you need me for something, my dear."

Cedrica sat, her mind racing as she reviewed all the ways she might have fallen short of Her Grace's high standards.

"When I saw you slip away with your Sun King, I thought you had found the path to your future, Cedrica, but since then, nothing. Or am I mistaken? Are you and your suitor keeping your agreement secret for some reason? You do not seem happy, dear child, and that simply will not do."

Cedrica opened her mouth to protest and then closed it again. Her Grace could not possibly know…

The duchess was silent, too, her face alive with interest, her head on one side as if she would listen forever, if that was how long it took for Cedrica to think of something to say.

"You do not understand, Your Gr—Aunt Eleanor."

"I would like to. I am an interfering old woman, my dear, but I wish you well, you know. And Monsieur Fournier, too. Yes, Cedrica, I did recognize him in my husband's Louis XIV costume and that ancient wig."

Suddenly, Cedrica found herself pouring the whole story into the duchess's sympathetic ears. Everything: the first unfortunate clashes, the growing attraction, the quiet times in the kitchen, the chef's surprising appearance at the costume party, and what came of it.

At length, the duchess gave her a hug and handed her a handkerchief. "So, he thinks you are far above him and is being noble about it."

Cedrica, who had somehow arrived on the rug at Her Grace's feet and was weeping into the noble lady's gown, looked up in surprise. "Is that what he is doing?"

"Yes, of course. Silly romantic boy."

Cedrica blotted her eyes and blew her nose. The duchess did not sound disapproving. Quite the contrary. "You do not mind? You do not think I would be marrying beneath me?"

"Does it matter what I think, my dear? Unless you are thinking of the dowry Aldridge promised?"

"I do not care about the dowry. Monsieur Fournier has plans… But, Aunt Eleanor, I care about your good opinion."

The duchess said nothing, smiling gently, one brow slightly arched.

Cedrica felt as she had in the village schoolroom when suddenly she knew the answer to a question that had eluded her for days. "But not as much as I care about Monsieur Fournier. I am sorry if you disapprove, Aunt Eleanor, but I will marry him if he will have me."

The duchess beamed with all the delight of a dedicated teacher. "Excellent. You do realize that you will have to ask him, Cedrica? Men can be so foolish." She shook her head fondly. "Off you go. This is a quiet time in the kitchen, is it not? Take your Monsieur Fournier for a walk. If any problems arise while you and Esther are occupied, I am sure I shall manage."

Cedrica hesitated a moment more and then startled them both with an impulsive hug. "Thank you, Aunt Eleanor."

In the kitchen, she went straight to his side before she lost her nerve.

"Monsieur Fournier," she said, "I need a word with you. Will you spare me a moment, please?"

Monsieur Fournier said nothing but nodded and gave the ladle he was holding to his assistant. Cedrica looked back as she led him out of the kitchen and along the passage that led to the outside door. He was frowning, but he still followed.

She stopped just inside the door and helped herself to one of the warm serviceable coats. His frown had given way to puzzlement, but he shrugged into one of the other coats and continued to follow her around the house and across the short bridge to the sleeping rose garden in which they had kissed.

He held back when she made straight for the arbor and sat down, and he shook his head, his eyes wary and alarmed, when she patted the bench beside her. Oh, dear. Was she about to make an enormous fool of herself?

Cedrica swallowed against the sudden constriction in her throat. "Monsieur Fournier…" What did one say? The etiquette guides for young ladies gave no instructions for such an occasion. "You cannot be unaware that I have come to hold you in the highest esteem…"

But he was shaking his head. "Non. No. *Cherie*, you must not. You pay me a great compliment, but I cannot." Through a film of tears, she saw him backing away. "I will not. Ah, *cherie*, do not cry." Two steps and he was kneeling at her feet, attempting to dry her eyes with the corner of his apron. "You would grow to hate yourself and me if I dishonored you so."

Suddenly, she was angry. "How dare you decide what dishonors me? To marry out of my class is a dishonor? You are very wrong! Even if I belonged in this frivolous world, you would be wrong. Condemn me to a cold and lonely life if you do not love me as I have come to love you," she caught a long shuddering breath, "but do not dare pretend you do it for my sake."

He was staring at her as if she had grown a second head. "Marry?" he asked.

"Of course 'marry.' What did you think I was…? Marcel! I am a vicar's daughter."

"Marry." He was grinning broadly. "I never imagined… Are you sure, Mademoiselle?" He had both her hands now and was smothering them with kisses. "I cannot give you the life you have here. I could perhaps manage a small apartment. I have money saved, but it would not be what you are used to."

"Marcel, this is not the life I am used to. I am the daughter of a vicar, who was himself the son of a clerk in a counting house. My ducal connections are so far back that I cannot even tell you how distant a cousin Lord Aldridge is. I am used to a life of counting pennies, and I am good at making do, I promise."

"You deserve to be dressed in silks and have maids to tend you."

"And be cold and lonely?" she asked again.

His response was a kiss, which was very satisfactory, and little was said in the arbor for some time.

Eventually, though, Cedrica returned to the topic of their future. "We must not dip into your savings for the restaurant, Marcel. When we have enough saved, we can open *Fournier's of London* and live above it in a little apartment."

"It could be three years, my own, and I do not wish to wait."

"I shall work, too," she assured him. "The duchess will let me stay, I think, and she pays me a salary and my keep."

"The duchess may turn you off if she knows you plan to marry a chef, Rica."

She smiled at her new nickname, the 'r' rolled over Marcel's tongue. "She knows. She sent me to you. I'll forfeit the dowry Lord Aldridge promised if I married a 'suitable' gentleman, but I told her I did not care about that, and she smiled. She will be happy for us, Marcel."

"Is it so?" he marveled.

"Yes. And I should return and tell her that we are betrothed. We are betrothed, are we not?"

"Yes, my Rica. I, Marcel Fournier, accept your proposal with a thankful heart." Marcel kissed her again to prove it, and it was some time later that Cedrica finally floated upstairs to tell her patroness her news.

Epilogue

London, August 1813

Fournier's *of London* had been open for three weeks, three weeks in which the numbers of diners had grown nightly until they needed to take bookings and began to turn people away at the door.

Tonight, though, no bookings had been accepted and nor would casual diners be able to penetrate into the elegant interior, where polished wood, crisp white linen, shining silver, and sparkling crystal waited for the few privileged guests.

And tonight, welcoming the diners would not be the task of the *maître d'hôtel* who usually managed the dining room while the proprietor controlled the kitchen.

Tonight, Marcel had left his chief assistant in charge of the final preparations. Tonight, Monsieur Fournier himself would greet his patrons, and not alone. For tonight, the restaurant, normally a sanctuary for gentlemen, would be entertaining women, and not only women, but ladies. Including Cedrica, who was waiting at the door.

Had it been less than a year since she had written to her father's noble relative in a last desperate bid to keep the bishop from locking the poor man up? How things had changed!

Here was the biggest change of all: her husband, looking splendid in a black dress coat and knee breeches. He slipped an arm around her waist and kissed the top of her head. "Are you nervous, cherie?"

"Proud, Marcel. I am looking forward to showing our investors what we have done."

He turned with her, surveying the largest of five dining rooms with satisfaction. Here, they could host up to one hundred diners at a time, with tables that could be divided or put together to suit the convenience of the patrons, from single diners to large banquets. The smallest of the rooms accommodated eight with comfort and could be configured for smaller groups.

Tonight, they would be using one of the medium-sized rooms, for tonight, they welcomed the friends who had taken shares in the restaurant.

It had been Lord Aldridge's idea. When Cedrica first realized that he planned to pay the dowry he had promised, she voiced her decision to split it between buying care for her father and helping Marcel pay for the restaurant, but Aldridge advised her to think again.

"The Grenfords owe your father a duty of care," he assured her. "Invest in the restaurant by all means, but not only in the restaurant. You also need a separate income. I suggest money in the Funds for security and then some other ventures that will give a greater return. You must think of your long-term security, cousin."

Cedrica had quizzed Marcel on his plans and then spent hours collecting figures and doing sums. "But we will need all that money if we are to open this year."

"We could work another year," Marcel suggested, "or open a lesser establishment."

"Or accept investors," Aldridge suggested. "You and Cedrica to hold the majority share, and no one else with more than…" He pursed his lips as he considered, "five percent. You would have my support. I am confident you will make me money."

Her Grace agreed, and so did the Laceys and the Suttons and others. In no time at all, it seemed, they had the funds to make over a building to Marcel's high standards, the rental on a comfortable home nearby, and investments in the Funds, Aldridge's cousin's trading company, a woolen mill in Manchester, and a canal building enterprise.

Less than two months after the end of the house party where it all started, Monsieur Marcel Fournier and Mademoiselle Cedrica Grenford were married. Twice. Once according to English practice and law and again in a small comfortable parlor off the side of the local Roman Catholic chapel.

And now Monsieur and Madame Fournier would say thank you to those who made it possible.

"It looks well," Marcel decided. "And the dinner, the dinner, my Rica, will be the most magnificent they have ever tasted."

Cedrica smiled. He said that every night, and every night, his guests assured him it was true.

Out in the hall, the restaurant door opened, and they could hear the *portier* greeting the first arrivals. In moments, it seemed, they were surrounded by cheerful friends, the men slapping Marcel on the back and congratulating him on making them all rich, the women kissing Cedrica on the cheek and gently scolding her for being too busy to meet friends for tea.

"Mama and I brought you a present," Aldridge said. "I left it in the hall. Just one moment." He left the room and returned a moment later with a long, flat, oblong shape wrapped in silk and tied with ribbon, which he handed to the duchess.

"We wanted to give you something useful but unusual, something that would always remind you of Hollystone Hall," she said.

Marcel, seated beside Cedrica, lifted her hand and kissed it. "I have a wonderful *souvenir* of that house party, Your Grace," he said.

The duchess smiled. "Indeed you do. To remind you of us, then, Monsieur. We consulted with Mrs. Pearce, and she suggested that this might be suitable."

What on earth could it be? Cedrica and Marcel took one end of the parcel each and began to untie ribbons. When Marcel cleared his end of the silk and saw the box within, he began to laugh. Cedrica was still mystified until she finished unwrapping and was able to open the box and see the pearwood mold within, the one with the dolphin shapes that had caused such contention.

"Look, Marcel, at last you will be able to make your ice tower!"

Leave it to Aldridge to have the last word, as he raised his glass of wine. "Ladies and gentlemen, I give you Fournier's of London. May it, and its proprietors, be a towering success."

THE END

This story first appeared in *Holly and Hopeful Hearts*, an anthology by the Bluestocking Belles. Many of the characters populating the background have their own stories in that book. In particular, Lady Sophia appears in *The Bluestocking and the Barbarian*, Esther Baumann in *An Open Heart*, by Caroline Warfield, and Lady Grace in *A Kiss for Charity* by Sherry Ewing.

Jude Knight would like your help

Book reviews help readers to find books, and authors to find readers. Please consider writing a review for *A Suitable Husband*, even a couple of sentences telling people what you liked (or didn't like) about it. Reviews can be posted on Goodreads and on most eretailers websites. For links to this book on those sites, see the *A Suitable Husband* page on my website: http://judeknightauthor.com/books/a-suitable-husband/

News and special offers

Subscribe to Jude's newsletter for information about publication dates and more. As a subscriber, you will receive advance information about release dates and special price periods as well as exclusive, subscriber-only special offers. Jude sends a newsletter six times a year. New subscribers receive a link to a page full of free short stories and novellas to download as ebooks.

You will find a subscription link at http://judeknightauthor.com

Acknowledgements

Thank you to the prizewinner, who gave Cedrica her name, and to the Bluestocking Belles who gave her a place to be and a job to do.

As always, a special thank you to my husband, without whose support I would probably forget to eat when I get stuck in the early nineteenth century, and to my sister Sue, who is always my first reader.

Bluestocking Belles

The Belles are eight very different writers united by a love of history and a history of writing about love. From sweet to steamy, from light-hearted fun to dark tortured tales full of angst, from London ballrooms to country cottages to the sultan's seraglio, one or more of the Belle's will have a tale to suit your tastes and mood.

The Belle's blog, *The Teatime Tattler*, publishes at least twice weekly, with exclusive news, interviews, and scandals set in and around the Regency.

The Belles have committed to publishing at least one box set per year. Proceeds from some of the Belles' joint projects go to the Malala Fund, to support education for young bluestockings around the world.

Find the Bluestocking Belles online:
www.BluestockingBelles.net/
Friend us on Facebook:
www.facebook.com/BellesinBlue
Follow us on Twitter:
@BellesInBlue

Malala Fund

The Bluestocking Belles have chosen the Malala Fund as the charity we support, and to which we donate communal royalties. Periodically, we take on projects intended to directly support this cause, which exemplifies our personal values and intentions: the right of girls and women to do whatever they choose with their lives.

For more information about the Malala Fund and the founder, Malala Yousafzai, winner of the 2014 Nobel Peace Prize, go to www.Malala.org

Holy and Hopeful Hearts

When the Duchess of Haverford sends out invitations to a holiday house party and a Twelfth Night ball, those who respond know that Her Grace intends to raise money for her favourite cause and promote whatever matches she can.

Eight assorted heroes and heroines set out with their pocketbooks firmly clasped and hearts in protective custody. Or are they?

Jude has two stories in Holy and Hopeful Hearts: *A Suitable Husband,* and *The Bluestocking and the Barbarian.*

Published books

See the excerpts page on Jude's website for first chapters of all the following stories. http://judeknightauthor.com/excerpts/

Candle's Christmas Chair

When Viscount Avery comes to see the best invalid chair maker in the southwest of England he does not expect to find Minerva Bradshaw, the woman who rejected him three years earlier. Or did she? Older and wiser, he wonders if there is more to the story.

For three years, Min Bradshaw has remembered the handsome guardsman who courted her for her fortune. She **didn't** expect him in her workshop, and she certainly **doesn't** intend to let him fool her again. Even if he is handsomer and more charming than ever.

Gingerbread Bride: A novella in the Golden Redepenning series

Lieutenant Rick Redepenning has been saving his admiral's intrepid daughter from danger since their formative years, but today, he faces the gravest of threats—the damage she might do to his heart. How can he convince her to see him as a suitor, not just a childhood friend?

Travelling with her father's fleet has left Mary Pritchard ill-prepared for London Society, and prey to the machinations of false friends. When she strikes out on her own to find a more suitable locale to take up her solitary spinsterhood, she finds adventure, trouble, and her girlhood hero, riding once more to her rescue.

Gingerbread Bride is a novella in *The Golden Redepennings* series and was first published in the box set *Marriage, Mistletoe, and Mayhem.*

Farewell to Kindness: Book 1 of The *Golden Redepennings*

Hidden from the earl who hunts them, Anne and her sisters have been accepted into the heart of a tiny rural village. Until another earl comes visiting.

Rede lives to avenge the deaths of his wife and children. After three long years of searching, he is closing in on the ruthless villains who gave the orders, and he does not hope to survive the final encounter. Until he meets Anne.

As their inconvenient attraction grows, a series of near fatal attacks draws them together and drives them apart. When their desperate enemies combine forces, Anne and Rede must trust one another to survive.

A Raging Madness: Book 2 of *The Golden Redepennings*

Ella survived an abusive and philandering husband, in-laws who hate her, and public scorn. But she's not sure she will survive love. It is too late to guard her heart from the man forced to pretend he has married such a disreputable widow, but at least she will not burden him with feelings he can never return. She prays he will learn to tolerate her.

Alex understands his supposed wife never wishes to remarry. And if she had chosen to wed, it would not have been to him. He should have wooed her when he was whole, when he could have had her love, not her pity. But it is too late now. She looks at him and sees a broken man. He hopes she will learn to bear him.

In a masquerade of marriage, Ella and Alex soon discover they are more well-matched than they thought possible. But then the couple's blossoming trust is ripped apart by an enemy determined to destroy them both. Two lost souls must together face the demons of their past to save their lives and give their love a future.

A Baron for Becky

Becky is the envy of the courtesans of the demi-monde—the indulged mistress of the wealthy and charismatic Marquis of Aldridge. But she dreams of a normal life; one in which her daughter can have a future that does not depend on beauty, sex, and the whims of a man.

Finding herself with child, she hesitates to tell Aldridge. Will he cast her off, send her away, or keep her and condemn another child to this uncertain shadow world?

The devil-may-care face Hugh shows to the world hides a desperate sorrow; a sorrow he tries to drown with drink and riotous living. His years at war haunt him, but even more, he doesn't want to think about the illness that robbed him of the ability to father a son. When he dies, his barony will die with him. His title will fall into abeyance, and his estate will be scooped up by the Crown.

When Aldridge surprises them both with a daring proposition, they do not expect love to be part of the bargain.

Revealed in Mist

Prue's job is to uncover secrets, but she hides a few of her own. When she is framed for murder and cast into Newgate, her one-time lover comes to her rescue. Will revealing what she knows help in their hunt for blackmailers, traitors, and murderers? Or threaten all she holds dear?

Enquiry agent David solves problems for the *ton*, but will never be one of them. When his latest case includes his legitimate half-brothers as well as the woman who left him months ago, he finds the past and the circumstances of his birth difficult to ignore. Danger to Prue makes it impossible.

Coming in 2017

Concealed in Shadow

The story of Prudence and David continues in *Concealed in Shadow*.

When Prue disappears with David's half-brother, he is determined she must have met with foul play, whatever interpretation Aldridge might put on it. But finding her again may mean choosing between his country and his woman.

Here are the first three paragraphs.

The ship had been at harbour for four days now, after a stormy passage from London. The sailor who brought their daily allocation of food and drink would not answer questions, but Prue guessed they were docked somewhere in Ireland. Certainly, the polyglot shouting that filtered into the ship's hold had been flavoured these last few days with the musical lilt of Gaelic, and of Irish-intoned English.

She and Gren were shackled to the same wall bolt, with enough play in the chains that they could reach the narrow bed, the bucket that did for amenities, and the food and drink their jailors periodically sent.

They had not seen those jailors since the day of their capture. Were Wharton and Jo Palmer still aboard? Had Aldridge raised the alarm? Would David be able to find trace of them? Prue fretted away the long hours wondering.

The Realm of Silence: Book 3 of *The Golden Redepennings*

Susan Cunningham's carefully managed life spirals out of control when her daughter Amy disappears from a select ladies' academy in Cambridge. Susan will do anything to find the missing fifteen year old, even accept help from Gil Rutledge, who once made her childhood miserable and yet stirs her as her deceased husband never did.

Gil seizes the chance to pursue the runaway schoolgirl up the Great North Road. It's a holiday from suffocating responsibilities he never wanted and is ill-prepared to manage—care of his mother and sisters, his dead brother's bankrupt estate. Most of all it's the chance to spend time with the only woman he has ever loved.

Catching up with Amy is merely the start. To save her, Susan and Gil must stand together against French spies and prisoners of war, English radicals, the British army and navy, and their own families. And even risk their hearts.

The Bluestocking and the Barbarian (first published in November 2016 in *Holly and Hopeful Hearts*)

James must marry to please his grandfather, the duke, and to win social acceptance for himself and his father's other foreign-born children. But only Lady Sophia Belvoir makes his heart sing, and to win her, he must invite himself to spend Christmas at the home of his father's greatest enemy.

Sophia keeps secret her *tendre* for James, Lord Elfingham. After all, the whole of Society knows he is pursuing the younger Belvoir sister, not the older one left on the shelf after two failed betrothals.

The Bluestocking and the Barbarian is Book 1 in Children of the Mountain King

With Mariana Gabrielle

Never Kiss a Toad

[A Victorian romance continuing family stories begun in the various Regency books of Jude Knight and Mariana Gabrielle.] David "Toad" Northope, heir to the Duke of Wellbridge and rogue in the mould of his infamous father, knows Lady Sarah "Sal" Grenford, daughter of the once-profligate Duke of Haverford, will always hold his heart.

But when the two teens are caught in bed together by their horrified parents, he is sent away to finish school on the Continent, and she is thrown into the depths of her first London Season.

Can two reformed rakes keep their children from making the same mistakes they did? The dukes decide keeping them apart will do the trick, so as the children reach their majority, Toad is put to work at sea, learning to manage his mother's shipping concern, and

Sal is taken to the other side of the world, as far from him as possible.

How will Toad and Sal's love withstand long years of separation, not to mention nasty lies, vicious rumours, attractive other suitors, and well-meaning parents who threaten to destroy their future before it has begun?

(*Never Kiss a Toad* is being published one episode at a time on Wattpad, and will be published complete as an ebook some time in 2017 or 2018.

Connect with Jude Knight

Jude Knight writes stories to transport you to another time, another place, where you can enjoy adventure and romance, thrill to trials and challenges, uncover secrets and solve mysteries, and delight in a happy ending. Meet strong determined heroines, heroes who can appreciate a clever capable woman, villains you'll love to loathe, and all with a leavening of humour.

Follow Jude on Twitter
Like Jude on Facebook
Subscribe to Jude's blog
Subscribe to Jude's newsletter
Follow Jude on Goodreads

www.ingramcontent.com/pod-product-compliance
Lightning Source LLC
Chambersburg PA
CBHW030755110726

47900CB00008B/2623